DUNKIN' Soaring Slammer

Andrew Einspruch

illustrated by Peter Foster

SuPa DOOPERS

sundance

For information regarding permission, write to:
Sundance Publishing
234 Taylor Street
Littleton, MA   01460

Published by
Sundance Publishing
234 Taylor Street
Littleton, MA   01460

Copyright © text Andrew Einspruch
Copyright © illustrations Peter Foster
Project commissioned and managed by
Lorraine Bambrough-Kelly, The Writer's Style
Cover and text design by Marta White

First published 1996 by
Addison Wesley Longman Australia Pty Limited
95 Coventry Street
South Melbourne 3205 Australia
Exclusive United States Distribution: Sundance Publishing

ISBN 0-7608-0765-5

Printed In Canada

CONTENTS

CHAPTER 1

The Flying Gnats — Lost in Last Place *5*

CHAPTER 2

Hot Shot vs. Hot Shot *17*

CHAPTER 3

Showdown *35*

CHAPTER 1

THE FLYING GNATS —
LOST IN LAST PLACE

Our team was the Gnats. The Flying Gnats.

We were the pits. The worst. We were rock bottom in a league of twenty teams. A herd of yaks in snowshoes probably could have beaten us.

But that was before Darrin.

JELLY BEAN

DINGO

BLADES

OZONE

The Sauce (that's Jimmy) saw Darrin first.
We call Jimmy "the Sauce" because he's got red
hair, like tomato sauce. All of us Gnats have
nicknames, like Loose, Bottle, and Choko.
I'm Ozone.

One Tuesday, we were sitting next to the practice court at lunchtime. The Sauce took a bite of his sandwich and said, "Some new kid moved in with old Mrs. Brinson."

"Who cares?" Bottle slurped his drink.

"Saw him bump his head on the door frame going in."

Loose scraped a last bit of cake with his finger. "What's his name?"

"Dunno. He didn't come back out."

That night we lost 51–9 to the next worst
team in the league, the Raging Rockets.
Choko was our top scorer. Four points.
I didn't score any. I usually didn't.

Coach Petersen yelled at us afterwards. "Men. No team in this league ever lost *every* game in a season. We have one more chance. Saturday."

Choko dropped his sneakers with a thud. "Sure. Like we're going to beat the Hoopsters."

They were the best. Not only had they won every game, they'd creamed the other teams by at least fifteen points.

As I walked home past the courts,
I saw the new kid. He was taller
than my dad. For ten minutes, he
sank basket after basket.

"Hey!" I called through the fence. "Don't you
ever miss?"

"Try not to," he said, swishing another.

I stood under the goalpost and bounced the ball back to him. "The guys call me Ozone."

"Darrin."

"Who do you play for?"

"No one. Mom and I just moved here from Los Angeles. Dad stayed behind."

"Want to be a Flying Gnat?"

"Gnats fly alright, but they don't go to the net."

"We don't play basketball too good either. We could use some help."

"Yeah? Well, maybe. Wanna play one-on-one?"

It was more like one-on-nothing. Darrin whooped me 21–3. The funny thing was, those three points were some of the best baskets I ever scored, and it was two points more than normal. Something about Darrin made me play my best.

But even better than scoring was watching Darrin
dunk the winner. It was a monster dunk!

"Wow! I've only seen Bernie Philps do that."
Bernie was the reason the Hoopsters were
number one.

Darrin bounced the ball. "I've been working on it."

"Look, I've gotta go," I said. "We practice in the
gym after school. See you there?"

Darrin shrugged.

That night I dreamed I was standing near center court. The crowd roared, which was weird, because no one comes to our games and they certainly don't cheer. Everything was spinning around, and all I could see was the game clock ticking toward zero.

I woke up sweating.

CHAPTER 2

HOT SHOT VS. HOT SHOT

At practice the next day, there was no sign of
Darrin. The guys were hopeless. Loose could
barely dribble. The Sauce tripped over his
shoelaces, and I couldn't even hit the
backboard. We knew we'd get clobbered by
the Hoopsters, so why bother practicing?

When Bottle missed his tenth layup in a row, he said, "Why don't we just give up?"

That's when Darrin showed up. Everyone stopped. In the doorway, with the bright afternoon light behind him, he looked like a shadow in the middle of the sun.

I stepped forward. "Coach, guys, this is Darrin. I said he could be a Gnat. That's okay isn't it?"

"Why would he want to be?" muttered Loose.

Coach Petersen looked Darrin over. "Go to school here?"

"Yep. Start tomorrow."

"Grab a ball, then."

It was just like when the two of us played one-on-one.

With Darrin there, every Gnat seemed
to get a little bit better. Loose dribbled
the ball a few more times before he lost
it. The Sauce stole a pass before he
tripped. Bottle dropped in a layup.
Even I *almost* sank a basket.

Darrin, however, was incredible. He
swished baskets from all over the court.

Just before we finished, he grabbed
a pass, leaped and jammed the ball
through the hoop. Choko yelled,
"Yesssss! It's Dunkin' Dazza!"

That's when Darrin really became
a Gnat. When he got his nickname.

We left practice feeling different. Pulling on my jacket, I figured out what it was. For the first time all season, we had something.

Hope.

At Burger Barn the next day, Darrin, Bottle, Loose, and I were ordering when Bernie Philps and some Hoopsters shoved in front of us.

"Hey losers, who's the geek?" Bernie asked, pointing at Darrin.

Bottle rolled his eyes. "Darrin, meet Bernie Philps, legend in his own mind."

Bernie grabbed Bottle's shirt. "Watch it, Snottle."

"Ooh, shoes! What shoes!" said Loose, pointing at Bernie's chunky, purple and black high-tops.

Bernie dropped Bottle and turned to Loose. "Shut up, Goose. Jumptronics are for winners. You don't deserve to even look at them."

"Come on guys," I said, "my appetite's gone."

We walked away. It was easier than getting in a fight. Darrin, who hadn't said anything, glanced back. "Is he always so nice?"

"Yep. That's his usual charm," said Loose.

Bottle turned around. "Yo! Bernadette! Know what? Darrin here makes you look like you play basketball in your mom's high heels."

"Sure. And Ozone's Santa Claus."

"Ho. Ho. Ho."

That afternoon we had practice again. With two days to go, we didn't really think we could win, even with Darrin. Still, we might keep from embarrassing ourselves.

"Teamwork men," said Coach Petersen during a break. "That's the key. No one can do it by himself."

It was odd. Darrin never said much; he just practiced hard. He assumed we'd be in the right place at the right time to take a pass or grab a rebound. For the first time all year, the Gnats played something like basketball.

Three of us stayed after practice to work on free throws. I was the worst. They call me Ozone because of all the air balls I chuck. I've never sunk two free throws in a row. Ever.

"You know what I think about when I shoot a free throw?" Darrin said after I missed another.

"What?"

"Nothing."

"Nothing?"

"Yeah. I tell myself there's no one watching. There's no one here but me. Me, the ball, the hoop. Then, before I shoot, I picture the ball swishing through the net."

I was about to try it when Bernie turned up with six Hoopsters. He picked up a ball, bounced it, then spun it on his middle finger.

"So, the new geek's a Frying Gnat. Bad choice, bonehead. You've joined basketball's no-hoper city."

We just stood there.

Bernie walked forward and drop-kicked the ball at Darrin, who caught it.
"Well, geek-face. I've brought my mother's high heels," he said pointing to his Jumptronics. "Let's settle this right now. One-on-one. It'll save you the trouble of showing up Saturday."

Darrin bounced the ball back.
"Not interested."

Bernie stepped closer and threw it again.
"Then you're a loser. You've got no
game."

Darrin tossed it back. "Not interested."

Bernie nodded and two Hoopsters lifted
Bottle by the forearms. Bernie threw the
ball at Darrin, hard.

Bottle bit his lip. "You jerk, I — ow!
Let me go you stupid — ouch!"

"Put him down."

"First to twenty-one?"

"Put him down!"

Bernie nodded and the Hoopsters dropped
Bottle. Darrin shook his head, slowly walking
toward half-court.

It was the first time I'd seen Darrin against
someone who could actually play. But something
was wrong. Bernie chewed him up and spit him
out. Stealing the ball, running past him, faking
him out, charging through him, Bernie sank
point after point. Darrin fumbled around,
missing shots I'd seen him make a dozen times.
Bernie outmuscled and outplayed him.

Until it was 20–6.

Bernie relaxed, sure he'd won. But when Darrin next took the ball, he gave me a little nod, then he blasted off like a space shuttle. He blew past Bernie and tossed in a layup. Bernie took the ball but Darrin covered him like an octopus, swatting away every shot. No one, ever since we were kids, had *ever* shut down Bernie so completely.

Darrin made eleven straight points.

Then he gave me that nod again. Bernie put up a shot that seconds before Darrin would have blocked. It bounced off the rim. Bernie elbowed Darrin, jumped, snagged the ball, and stuffed it through the hoop.

"Yes!" he yelled. "Geek Destroyer strikes again!"

"Way to go, Bernie," said a Hoopster.

"Come on, guys," Bernie said. "See you, geek."

When they were gone, Darrin wiped a hand across his brow and bounced the ball to me. "Let's have another free throw."

I missed.

CHAPTER 3

SHOWDOWN

The next morning, everyone was talking about Bernie and Darrin. Bernie said he'd "aced the geek," but people knew about Darrin's eleven-point streak.

"How'd they find out?" I asked Bottle.

"I might've mentioned something on the bus."

"Get real, Bottle," said the Sauce. "You practically had a T-shirt made up."

At recess, everyone talked as if the Gnats had some secret weapon. Nobody thought we'd actually beat the Hoopsters, but they wondered if Darrin was even half as good as Bottle said.

By lunchtime, Bernie was steamed that
Darrin was taking him out of the limelight.
"I blitzed him," he said again, too loudly.

From the other side of Burger Barn, someone
yelled, "I'd like to see a rematch, Berno."

Someone else said, "Hey, Darrin, you playing in
the game tomorrow?"

Darrin looked up from his sandwich and nodded.

Bernie stood up. "The Fried Gnats don't stand a
chance."

"What about those eleven points, Bernice?" said Bottle, leaning back in his chair.

"You guys are history. We'll blast you to Mars."

"And if you don't?"

Bernie stuck out his chest. "If we don't beat you by twenty, I'll burn my Jumptronics." The room buzzed. "But. . ." The room hushed. "Lose by twenty-one or more, and Snottle is my slave for a month."

Bottle jumped to his feet. "You're on, Bernadette."

At practice that afternoon, everyone was
nervous. Darrin left early to help his
grandmother with something, leaving the rest
of us feeling like a mouth without front teeth.
Darrin or no Darrin, Bernie's Jumptronics
were safe. And Bottle was headed for slavery.

The game started at 2:00 P.M. but by 1:30 the gym was wall-to-wall with kids, plus a few parents (including mine). Before the game, Coach Petersen simply said, "Play hard. Play like a team."

Bernie outjumped Darrin for the tip-off, but Choko came up with the ball. He dribbled down the court, passed it to Darrin, who looked at the basket.

The Hoopsters had two guys on him, so, much to my surprise, he bounced it to me. I guess I didn't think I'd be doing much during the game, since I never did. Without even thinking, I put up a jump shot from the three-point line.

Swish.

I was stunned. I'd scored the game's first goal. Already I was two points over my average.

"Way to go, Ozo!" Loose said, slapping high-fives.

"Fluke," sneered Bernie.

I didn't score again that half, but Darrin did. Lots. So did Choko, but Bernie, and a couple of Hoopsters were too hot and at halftime they led 39–29. As expected, it was a battle between the centers. Bernie's muscle controlled the inside, but he picked up four fouls on the way. Darrin was quicker, making most of his shots from outside.

The third quarter was about the same. We played better than we had all season, but the Hoopsters went ahead by seventeen.

Everything changed at the
beginning of the fourth quarter.
The Sauce took a pass and
headed up for a layup. Bernie
jumped to block the shot, but
slapped him on the cheek instead
The referee blew his whistle and
pointed. Foul trouble.

"Time out!" yelled the Hoopsters' coach.
When they came back on court, Bernie wasn't
with them.

The Sauce sank two free throws, then stole a pass from a Hoopster guard. His jump shot bounced in. Suddenly, the Hoopsters' thirteen-point lead didn't seem impossible.

The next ten minutes belonged to Choko and Darrin. They were everywhere. Each basket brought cheers from the crowd. Without Bernie, the Hoopsters drooped like a two-day-old balloon. With three minutes to go, Darrin sank a three-pointer. We Gnats had pulled to within four points, and the crowd leaped to its feet.

"Time out!" This time it was Coach Petersen.

Bottle walked past Bernie on his way to the bench and sniffed the air. "Isn't that the smell of melting Jumptronics?"

"Bottle, get over here," yelled Loose.

Every one of us knew the basketball shoes were no longer the point. We wanted something that four days before we never would have dreamed — a win over the Hoopsters.

Bernie came back in. The Hoopsters started to stall to run out the clock. "Full-court press!" shouted Coach Petersen.

The Hoopsters passed the ball, using up the shot clock, but missed from the baseline. Bernie grabbed the rebound, and they kept control. Again the shot clock wound down, and the Hoopsters took a last-second shot. It swirled around the inside of the hoop and popped out.

Loose caught the ball
and fed Darrin a pass.
He worked down the
court, moved to his
right, and arched in a
perfect skyhook. We
were two points away.
The crowd chanted,
"Dazza! Dazza!"

The Hoopsters brought down the ball slowly, brushing off our full-court press. The clock showed twenty-five seconds. Bernie took a pass, leaped over Darrin, and tried a dunk shot. Instead of jamming it into the basket, the ball smacked the rim and flew toward half-court.

To me.

"Foul him! Foul him!" yelled Bernie.

A Hoopster ran up and pushed me.
The referee whistled the foul. "Penalty
situation. One-and-one."

Bernie figured I'd miss the free throw,
they'd get the rebound, and that'd be
the game. He was probably right.

Stepping up to the foul line, I heard
my parents yell, "You can do it."
A lump like a golf ball stuck in my
throat, and my hands were clammy.
Hoopsters on and off the court jeered
"Air ball! Aaaaaaaair ballllllll! Chuck
it in the ozone. Aaaaaaair ballllllll!"

I remembered what Darrin said about free
throws. In my mind, I made the gym go quiet.
There was just me, the ball, and the hoop.
Me. Ball. Hoop. I saw the path it would take
and imagined sinking the shot. I took a breath,
hefted the ball, and let it fly.

Wooosh! Perfect.

The crowd cheered. You could barely hear the referee say, "Second shot," as he handed the ball back. Oh no, I thought. Never, ever, not in a game, not in practice, not by myself in our backyard — never had I sunk two free throws in a row. My stomach knotted.

I bounced the ball once. For an instant, I looked to the left. There was Darrin, crouched, ready, watching me. His eyes did not hold hope. They did not encourage. They did not plead. Darrin simply looked at me like he knew I could do it. No questions. Again, I tried to make the gym quiet and see another perfect shot.

The Hoopsters chanted, "Choke! Choke! Choke! Choke!"

The ball flew up, then down.
It bounced up off the rim. Ten
sweating bodies surged toward it.
The ball bounced on the rim a
second time and seemed to
hang forever.
It dropped through the net.
The crowd went berserk.
Twenty seconds left. Tie game.

The Hoopsters brought the ball into play. Bernie yelled, "Me! Give it to me!" He took a pass with fifteen seconds to go, dribbled twice, and leaped for the hoop.

It should have been an easy shot. No one was near enough to block it, and he jumped high enough. The only problem was, he didn't have the ball. Bottle had stolen it.

Choko took Bottle's pass, saw Darrin was covered, and threw up a wild shot. It bounced off the backboard and came right at me. So did two Hoopsters.

Everything seemed to move in slow motion, like
a movie. Through the legs of the oncoming
Hoopsters, I saw Darrin in front of Bernie, eyes
locked on me. I leaped as high as I could and
passed the ball, just as the Hoopsters knocked
me down. The gym whirled as I fell. I glimpsed
the clock: four seconds, three seconds . . .

Then I saw Darrin
again, face-to-face
with a snarling Bernie.
He faked right, moved
left, and leaped for the
basket, the ball in his
left hand. Bernie
jumped to block it,
but Darrin started to
spin around. The ball
slid from his left hand
to his right as he flew
toward the basket, his
back to the hoop. I
thought, he can't see
where he's going.

The final buzzer sounded, as Dunkin' Dazza jammed home a twisting, backwards, two-handed, over-the head, once-in-a-lifetime slam dunk.

The crowd exploded onto the court, and we hauled Darrin onto our shoulders.

I have to hand it to Bernie. After school on Monday, he offered to make good and burn his Jumptronics.

Bottle looked at him and shrugged. "Don't bother. Next year, you're going to really need those shoes."